THE HAIRY BEAR in his red UNDERWEAR

by Gladys Dorfman

Illustrated by
Gladys Dorfman and Roc Goudreau

Published in the United States by
Hannah Mae Enterprises, Inc.
P.O. Box 81143
Springfield, MA 01138-1143

Printed in the United States by Arrow Printing. Bemidji, Minnesota.

Publisher's Cataloging-in-Publication
(Provided by Quality Books, Inc.)

Dorfman, Gladys
The hairy bear in his red underwear/
by Gladys Dorfman. -- 1st ed.
p. cm.
SUMMARY: Two children have a day of fun at the circus, the fair and other places with their friend, a hairy bear in red underwear..
LCCN: 2002106247
ISBN: 0-9671111-4-5
1. Bears--Juvenile fiction. 2. Underwear--Juvenile fiction
[1. Bears--Fiction. 2. Underwear--Fiction. 3. Stories in rhyme.]
I. Title

PZ8.3.D7335Ha 2001 [E]
QBI02-701631

This book is dedicated to all the children who dream, pretend, create, and use their imaginations to venture to places they would like to go.

The sun was shining. It was a beautiful day.
We did not want to sit in the house all the long day.
We went down the stairs,
and there was the bear sitting in his chair
in his red underwear.

He put on his cap
and picked up his chair
and said, "Let us go outside
and get some fresh air."

Out the door we went with the hairy
bear with his chair in his red underwear.

"Let us go to the fair," said the hairy bear.
He had a map on his lap.
The hairy bear knew how to get to the fair.

We did not have to hike.
We went to the fair on our bikes.

When we got to the fair, everyone stared at the hairy bear in his red underwear.

We got on the merry-go-round, and the bear did not make a sound as the merry-go-round went around and around.
The merry-go-round is a fun place to be,
and a bear on a merry-go-round is a funny thing to see.

We got off the merry-go-round and went on the Ferris wheel.
You should never eat a meal before going on a Ferris wheel.
The Ferris wheel went up so high that we began to sigh.

We got off the Ferris wheel and went
on the roller coaster. That was a thrill!
We hung on tight and sat very still.

We got off the roller coaster
and ran to the water slide.
Down the slide we went, the two of us
with the bear in his red underwear.
When we got off the water slide,
everyone stared at the bear in his wet, red underwear.

We bought ice cream on a stick. It was fun to lick the ice cream on a stick. We were tired and wanted to take a nap, but the bear pulled out his map. "A circus would be a fun place to be," said the bear in his wet, red underwear.

To the circus we went
and found the big tent.
There were clowns with red noses,
and some even had roses.

Inside the tent was a clown.
"Sit down," said the clown with a frown.
"Please sit down."

So the bear sat down in a chair
as everyone stared at the sight of a bear
sitting down in a chair in his red underwear.
We found a seat and got something to eat.
There were elephants standing in line.
They did not seem to mind spending time standing in line.

There were lions sitting in chairs
and standing on stairs.
They did not seem to care
that they were sitting in chairs
and standing on stairs.

There were tigers leaping through rings
that looked like they were on fire.
The rings kept going higher and higher.

The bear got tired of sitting in a chair.
"Let us go outside," said the bear, "and get some fresh air."
Out the door we went with the bear in his red underwear.
There was a pail behind a rail.
The bear tried to put his head inside the pail.
His head turned red, and people stared.
They had never seen a bear
with red hair wearing red underwear.

"Come with me," said the bear with red hair and red underwear,
"to get some apples, peaches, and pears."

The bear climbed up a tree.
That was a funny thing to see,
a bear climbing up a tree.
He crawled out onto a branch.
That was a bad thing to do
because the branch snapped in two.
"Have no fear," said the bear
as his underwear began to tear.

Then down came the bear in his torn underwear.
That was quite a sight to see, a bear falling from a tree.
We gave the bear a hug and helped him out of the mud.

It was getting late, but we went to the lake.
We had a bar of soap on a rope.
The bear washed his hair
and his red underwear.
Then the bear put on his cap
and sat and sat and sat.

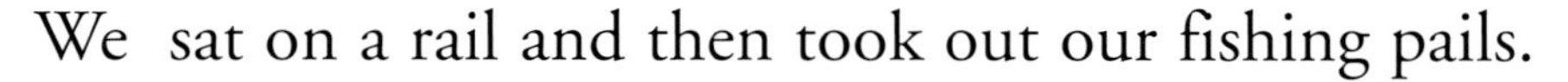

We sat on a rail and then took out our fishing pails.
We baited our hooks as the bear looked.
Then into the water he went. He did not miss.
He caught fish one by one until he caught twenty-one.
The bear did not move like a snail as he put his fish into a pail.
We saw a squirrel holding a pail, hanging by his tail on a rail.
Now that is a sight that you might never see,
a squirrel with a pail, hanging by his tail on a rail.

Then it began to rain.
We saw no harm.
We ran into a barn.

There was hay in the barn. We played in the hay,
but we did not stay the rest of the day.
There was one more thing we wanted to do,
and that was to go to the zoo.
"No, no," said the bear, "They might keep me there."
When the rain had stopped,
we saw no harm in leaving the barn.

When we got home and reached the front gate, it was very late.
We went into the house and up the stairs.
We put the big hairy bear into his chair.

The bear sat in his chair, not moving a hair.
We stared and stared at the bear in his chair.
We fell asleep without even a peep.
Tomorrow will be another day
for us to go out and play.

Where would you like
to go with your
imaginary bear?